COLLAPSE

By Scott Carleton

All rights reserved. No part of this document may be reproduced or transmitted in any form, either by electronic or mechanical means including information storage and retrieval systems without the prior written permission of the publisher. The only exception is for a reviewer who may quote brief passages in the review.

This publication is presented to you for informational purposes only and is not a substitution for any professional advice. The contents herein are based on the views and opinions of the author and all associated contributors.

While every effort has been made by the author and all associated contributors to present accurate and up to date information within this document, it is apparent technologies rapidly change. Therefore, the author and all associated contributors reserve the right to update the contents and information provided herein as these changes progress. The author and/or all associated contributors take no responsibility for any errors or omissions if such discrepancies exist within this document.

The author and all other contributors accept no responsibility for any consequential actions taken, whether monetary, legal, or otherwise, by any and all readers of the materials provided. It is the reader's sole responsibility to seek professional advice before taking any action on their part.

Readers results will vary based on their skill level and individual perception of the contents herein, and thus no guarantees, monetarily or otherwise, can be made accurately. Therefore, no guarantees are made.

Copyright © 2013 Velocity House

ISBN: 978-1-62409-020-2

Dedication

for my family

Foreword

Everything you are about to read has already happened.

This book is fiction, and the characters in it are completely made up, the events this novella depicts have already occurred again and again around the world and even in the United States.

During the LA riots, which exploded after the Rodney King trial verdict, a man named Reginald Denny was dragged from his truck and beaten nearly to death because of the color of his skin. In those same riots, Korean immigrant shop-owners famously took to the roofs of the businesses with assault rifles, successfully defending their livelihoods from the roaming mobs.

During the Northeast Blackout of 2003, a massive power outage in the Northeast United States and portions of Canada left 45 million Americans and 10 million Canadians without power, some for several days. The blackout highlighted the weakness of the North American power grid and prompted many to worry about the grid's vulnerability to terrorist attack.

During Hurricane Katrina, a breakdown of emergency planning and emergency services left many stranded in the storm zone. Horror stories about poor conditions, violent crime, and rampant rape and looting began to circulate, especially around the Superdome (where displaced area residents were housed). Disaster aid was so ineffectual that many famous entertainers and pundits claimed the president "didn't care" about the predominantly black residents of the New Orleans area.

In the aftermath of "Super Storm Sandy," New Yorkers were still suffering a lack of food, power, and water days and even weeks after the storm ripped through the state, killing 125 people and doing 62 billion dollars in damage. A month after the disaster, New York and New Jersey were seeking nearly 80 billion dollars in aid -- aid that was very slow in coming.

During the Occupy Wall Street protests in late 2011, the "Occupy" encampment in New York City began breeding crime and disease in alarming measure. Special "rape tents" were set up where female denizens of the camp could go for greater safety from their fellow demonstrators. A respiratory disorder known as Zucotti Lung began to affect the camp-goers, while neighborhood businesses suffered from rampant crime and vandalism. Many local businesses closed -- some temporarily, and some for good.

The fact is we live in a world constantly beset by

natural disasters, emergencies, and even civil unrest and riots. Most of us do not consider these things and, on a day-to-day basis, we live lives of luxury and convenience. We take our power, our Internet connections, our portable electronic devices and smartphones, completely for granted. Many of us don't even own landlines any more. We count on electricity and electronics for all of our entertainment, information, and communications. Our jobs depend heavily on these things. Our children would not know what to do with their time without them. The average crowd of people features a high percentage of men and women whose chins are in their chests as they stare at their handheld wireless devices. We are totally dependent on infrastructures and modern conveniences that can be knocked out by something as simple as a brown-out during a heat wave.

Ask yourself: If you were stuck at home during a sudden blizzard, how much food do you have? If you went to the store to buy batteries during a power-outage and discovered the shelves bare, what would you do? What do you have stockpiled at home in terms of emergency supplies? If you needed to perform first aid, could you? If your children became sick but a state of emergency had declared "No Unnecessary Travel" was to take place, how would you cope?

Are you prepared at all for even a two- or three-day emergency? Could you deal with a power outage that lasted for even 48 hours?

What if your neighbors started to riot?

It's happened before.

Most of us simply can't picture these events, but they occur every day. Most of these occurrences are out of sight, out of mind, happening far away from our home state or in other countries entirely. Nobody wants to think an emergency or a period of civil unrest could happen to them... until the day it does.

The events in these pages are all drawn from real-life events. They're things that have actually occurred during other emergencies, when the unthinkable happened to people who thought it never could come to them. Read these pages and ask yourself what you would do in similar situations.

If you aren't prepared, the good news is that you still can be. The time to prepare for an emergency is before it happens. If you have the time to read and enjoy this adventure, you have the time to prepare yourself for the types of very realistic emergency scenarios it presents. You have a responsibility to protect yourselves and those you love -- people who count on you to defend and care for them.

Remember that this is fiction. What's happening to Matthew isn't happening to you, not yet.

But it could. And it could happen very soon.

It's only a matter of time.

Chapter 1

"Dios Mio, this heat" said Matthew Avery, rubbing the back of his neck with the bandanna he kept in his pocket.

"Did you turn into a polite day laborer when I wasn't looking?" asked Kepler.

Matthew held up a middle finger. "It's something my mother used to say. Unless you'd like to make some more racist jokes?"

"Jeez, all right, already," Kepler said, putting up one hand as if in surrender. "How long have we been sitting here, anyway?" He didn't look at Matthew as he spoke. He was instead staring, frustrated, at his smartphone, trying again and again to place a call with no success. Around them, the honking of horns from frustrated drivers was growing more frequent. Before them, the downtown street was jammed with cars, none of them moving.

"It's been at least two hours," Matthew said.

"I think we're going to be late getting back from lunch," said Kepler.

Matthew shot him his most irritated glare. It was ironic that only two and a half hours earlier he had been complaining about the temperature in their office building.

"Do you know, Daniel, that it's almost seventy-nine degrees in here?" Matthew had said.

"That's a real heat wave," Daniel had shot back over the flimsy fabric-covered wall that separated them. "Shouldn't you be used to the heat? Isn't always a hundred and whatever south of the border?" He never stopped typing at his computer; Matt could hear him clacking away at the keyboard with heavy fingers. You could always spot the ones who learned on a manual typewriter. He had described manual typewriters to his five-year-old daughter once, who could operate a tablet or a laptop computer with ease. She had told him he was silly. She told him that whenever she thought he was making things up.

"My mother was from Mexico," said Matthew. "It's not like I just crossed the border on the back of a lettuce truck." He stopped short of calling Kepler something ugly. He was accustomed to ignoring the man's politically incorrect jibes. "And I'm serious. The HVAC hasn't been right since the renovations last year. It is too cold downstairs and it is always too warm up here."

"And an icebox in the cubes by the stairwell," said Kepler. "Thank God, Matt. It means whenever Sara wears one of those tight tops you can see her—"

"You're going to get a visit from Human Resources," Matthew said, "if you don't stop talking like that."

"Be glad it isn't hotter," said Kepler, still typing. "The summer we've had. It's supposed to hit ninety-eight by this afternoon, according to my weather app." Kepler waved his smartphone over the wall of the cubicle.

"Don't remind me," said Matthew. He finished the file on which he was working, a market analysis for one of their largest clients. He had worked for Simmons Marketing for eight years; Kepler for seven. They were ostensibly friends but, truth be told, there was much about Daniel Kepler that rubbed Matthew the wrong the way. Moving his mouse to the "save" button, he clicked it.

Every light on the second floor went out.

"You have got to be kidding me!" Matthew shouted. The backup battery for his workstation did not work; it beeped loudly, but lost charge in only moments. Throughout the cubicles on the second floor, the outraged beeping of other backup units tolled in what was by now a too-familiar keening. Matthew silently willed the "save" process to complete before his machine lost power completely. The screen went dark. The windowless cubicle farm was now completely dark except for a pair of emergency battery lights over the fire exits. Matthew reached into his pocket, found his tactical flashlight, and switched it on.

"Did you lose anything?" said Kepler's voice in the darkness. It was closer than usual. Matthew swung the light over and Kepler flinched away. He had been leaning over the cubicle wall. "Hey! Watch it with that billion candle-power spotlight, Matt."

"It's sixty lumens," said Matthew. "It's old now. There are lots brighter on the market."

"You and your gadgets," said Kepler. "Come on, it's almost noon. We might as well go out to lunch. There's no telling how long it will take them to get the network back up, even if the power comes back on."

"This is getting ridiculous," said Matthew. The city had been experienced rolling blackouts all summer. These had increased in frequency in the last few weeks. It was at times like these, with the background noise of the building's ventilator fans hushed, that he could hear traffic on the downtown streets below. The last brown-out had affected most of the city for half an hour at the least. Matthew did not like to think of 200,000 people without power. Temperatures — and tempers — could only climb in conditions like those.

"Your tax dollars at work," said Kepler. "Come on. It's your turn to buy."

"I bought last time."

"Well it's my turn the next two times," said Kepler. "I'm broke until payday."

"I've heard that before," grumbled Matthew. "Do you think they'll have power at the mall?"

"They did last time," said Kepler. "I think maybe they have their own backup generators or something."

The thought of sitting in cool, air-conditioned comfort,

sipping an iced coffee, was as appealing as spending his lunch hour with Kepler was not. The two often worked together on projects, which made it necessary for them to spend working lunches together. Matthew disliked Kepler's tendency to leer at the young girls who passed by, to say nothing of his habit of hitting on waitresses.

But it was already getting hotter...

"All right," said Matthew. "But you're definitely buying the next time. And the time after that."

On the way down the stairs, which were lighted through floor-to-ceiling windows that spanned both stories, they ran into Gabriel Samms from Accounting.

"I can't take this heat," said Samms.

"We're headed out for lunch," said Kepler. "You want to come?"

"No," said Samms. "The last time the power was out the Italian place on Franklin was completely packed and some guy spilled his beer on me. I thought I was going to get punched in the face over it when I called him on it."

"We just thought you were an alcoholic," said Kepler, grinning.

"Very funny, Dan." He tried his phone again, to no success. He had checked it every few minutes since the blackout.

Now, after a couple of hours immobile in the downtown traffic jam, Kepler's sense of humor was grating on Matthew's nerves all the more. The worst part, Matt reflected, was not knowing what had caused the jam-up.

They had listened to the local AM radio station, hoping for a traffic update, but none had been forthcoming. Around them, foot traffic had increased as more and more people abandoned their vehicles. A high-end sneaker store to their right had drawn a large crowd of loiterers. They were a rough bunch, from the looks of them. All young, Hispanic males. Matthew didn't like what he was seeing at all. They wore gang colors.

He tried to call his wife to see if everything was okay at home. He would most likely have to work late to make up the time lost on his lunchtime misadventure. He frowned when the call failed. He and Kepler used different carriers, but both networks were down.

"Somebody up ahead there better be dead," Kepler said. "This is ridiculous. What are we, a third world nation?" Kepler's own mood had deteriorated since they had been forced to shut the car off to prevent it from overheating. That meant no air conditioning. The mall food court was starting to look like an oasis indeed.

"Daniel," said Matthew. He cocked his head and put one hand behind his ear. "Listen. Do you hear that?"

"Is that... thunder?" asked Kepler.

Then Matthew saw it: Up ahead, a group of Hispanic teenagers was working its way down the street. As the two men watched, one of the members of the group waved to the loiterers outside the shoe store. There were some traded shouts in Spanish and English. Apparently the thugs all knew each other.

Probably part of the same gang, Matthew thought.

"What is that noise?" Kepler asked.

Matthew's eyes snapped to the street outside the car. The Hispanic gang had produced a couple of baseball bats. He thought he saw the glint of a knife in yet another hand. As Matthew watched, one of the gang members smashed out the window of the shoe store. He realized, then, that the gang members had been smashing windows all down the street.

"Daniel," he said. He could feel the change in his own voice, could feel his testicles trying to crawl back up into his abdomen. He put his hand on his car door.

"What is it?"

"Get ready to run," said Matthew.

Chapter 2

The office was an oven by the time they reentered. The power was still out, which meant the electronic door locks did not work. Someone had propped open the front doors to permit employees to reenter the building.

"What did you say to those guys, man?" Kepler asked again. He held a bloody handkerchief to his face. The bleeding from his smashed nose had stopped on its own, which was a good sign, but Matthew knew he had made a mistake. In saving Kepler's life he had made the man look foolish and powerless. Kepler was the not the sort who would forget an insult like that.

Kepler had asked the same question through his bloody face as they finally crawled back through heavy traffic toward the office. State Troopers had come through on foot and by motorcycle, directing anyone who could leave downtown to return the way they had come. By the time the cops had arrived, the gang of looters had taken what they wanted from the shoe store and the bodega across the street, not to mention a wireless phone store on the corner. The cops had barely glanced at the stores except to make sure the employees inside were not injured.

The owner of the shoe store had been bloody as the cops led him out to a waiting ambulance. Even with the sirens and lights going, Matthew had watched with great concern as the ambulance struggled to push through the already clogged downtown traffic. He found himself wondering, in the hour it took to get back to the office, just how long the poor man had been made to wait to reach a hospital. Kepler and Matthew had their own problems, too. Several times they had nearly had a fender-bender as aggressive drivers bulled into the slow-moving line of cars.

It had been a near thing, especially with Kepler behind the wheel, when the thugs took notice of them. Matthew recognized the gang colors, of course. He had grown up around gangs in neighborhoods much poorer than the one in which his family now lived.

The gang members were targeting what Matthew's mother would have called "Anglos" — European whites. They were looking through the shop windows and, when they saw an employee or an owner who looked too pale to suit them, they smashed out his windows. Matthew could read the coiled anger in their body language. They wanted someone to resist them, wanted someone to challenge them. This would be all the provocation they would need, in their minds, to justify beating a man, perhaps to death. That must have been what happened to the shoe store owner. He must have stood up to them when they entered his shop, instead of simply letting them take what they wanted.

"This is bullshit," said Kepler. "I'm not letting any group of trash like them just bully everyone—"

"Daniel, no!" said Matthew. "Stop!"

Kepler didn't listen. He got out and immediately put himself in the path of the nearest of the thugs. Kepler was a big, fit man. He obviously thought he knew how to handle himself, and Matthew wouldn't want to take a punch from the man if he could help it. But these were street thugs. They didn't trade punches. If Kepler didn't get stabbed, he stood a good chance of getting stomped to death by the bunch of them.

"Walk away," Kepler growled. He fixed the gang member in front of him with a hard glare, puffing out his chest and drawing himself up to his full height. "Don't make me do something you won't like."

The gang member's jaw dropped. He turned to his buddies outside the shoe store, who traded similarly astonished glances. Then the thug's mouth split in a wide grin.

The gang members started laughing.

"Get a load of this crazy puto," said the thug. "Please don't hurt me, old man. I might die of fright on the way to the ground."

"You little punk—" Kepler had time to say, before the thug kneed him in the crotch. Kepler folded and the gang member threw a second knee into his face. Blood spurted on the sidewalk.

Stepping out of Kepler's car was the hardest thing Matthew had ever had to do. His mouth was dry and his hands shaking. He quickly grabbed Kepler and dragged him back a step, smiling and putting up one hand with his palm out.

"Hey, guys," he had said, feeling like he should be holding a hat between his hands. "Espíritu de mi alma! Man, it's hot today. It's good to see somebody's out having fun. Boy, he sure deserved that. You got him good. He never could take a punch."

"What's it to you?" the thug asked. He looked like he wasn't finished with Kepler.

"Hey, guys, no disrespect. Far from it. I have friends back in the old neighborhood," Matthew said. Under his breath he whispered to Kepler, "Don't say a word. Go back to the car and get in on the passenger side. Don't make eye contact with anyone. Go now."

"Get out of the way, cabrón," said a second of the thugs. "Get lost."

"No problem," said Matthew. "No problem. I just need to corral this fool so we can get back to work." He hoped Kepler was far enough away not to hear the exchange. He heard the car door open. Matthew made sure to keep his back turned to his coworker. "But maybe you can help me out. I'd like to buy you guys a drink." He held up forty dollars in folded twenties. "But I just need a small favor in return. My jodido coworker over there, man, you would not believe that guy. But he and I need to get to an important meeting, and we're going to be in enough trouble when we get there, we're so late. It's all I can do to keep that puto in line. Can you let him slink away, man? He's all talk, that one."

The gang members paused, eyeing the money in Matthew's hand. He was taking a big risk. They might decide that all of his money was preferable.

"Of course, if I see the policia," he said, "I'll be sure to tell them all about the sudden hailstorm that broke out these shop windows." He managed a conspiratorial wink. "Qué lástima! I'll be stuck in the office until late, dealing with this heat. Have some fun for me."

"Whatever, man," said the thug who had struck Kepler. He snatched the money from Matthew's hand. The gang members gave Kepler, sitting in the car, a moderately wide birth. They spat at him, making profane gestures as they passed.

"Don't say a word," Matthew hissed as he climbed back into the driver's seat. Kepler had started to put his trembling hand on his door handle again. His face was red with fury. "Don't," said Matthew. "They'll leave us alone if you don't screw it up. Don't give them a reason to come back."

By the time Matthew and Kepler got back to the

office, Matthew's desperation to speak to his wife, to make sure she and their daughter were safe, was mounting.

"So what did you say?" Kepler asked yet again. They entered Matthew's cubicle, with his tactical flashlight leading the way. Matthew went to the lower drawer of his filing cabinet, unlocked it, and removed a Nylon power-drill bag with a shoulder strap.

"I basically appealed to their sense of shared adversity," said Matthew.

"What do you mean?" Kepler dabbed at his nose. Some of his usual attitude was returning.

"I told them you were a jerk, implied that beating you would make trouble for me at work, and bribed them with beer money."

Kepler was silent for a long moment, absorbing that. "Since when do you speak Spanish like a gang member?"

"If I didn't know how from growing up," Matthew said, "I'd have learned. Maybe you've noticed that the country's not as pale as it once was. You'd be a fool not to learn a language, especially Spanish."

Kepler did not know what to say to that. He looked down at the bag, which Matthew was now unzipping. "What do you need a power drill for?"

"It's not a power drill," said Matthew. "It's just the bag for one. Blends in better."

Chris Smith, the Operations Manager, appeared at the side of the cubicle. "Everyone's cleared out," he told them. "You two are the last ones in the building."

"The doors were propped open," said Matthew. "Do you mean to tell me there's almost no one here and the building was left wide open? That's a terrible idea."

Smith shrugged. "I'll close them on the way out. Make sure you leave them locked when you go."

"The roads are jammed throughout the city," said Matthew. "You may not get far."

"I'm sure not staying here," said Smith. They heard his footsteps on the stairwell before the fire door closed behind him.

"What now?" said Kepler. He began chewing his fingernails. "What the hell are we gonna do? We can't go anywhere. We can't do anything. The streets are clogged and our phones don't work. And I'm freaking starved." He began pacing back and forth.

Matthew propped his flashlight on top of his monitor where it illuminated the bag. He began removing items from it. The first of these was a battery-powered emergency radio that incorporated a fluorescent lantern. He switched this one.

"What... what have you got there?"

"You might call it an office survival kit," said Matthew. "It has some things that are useful for times like these. Here." He took a granola bar from the kit and gave it to Kepler. In the light of the emergency radio-lantern, the shadows playing across Kepler's face made it look like a skull.

Kepler grunted and tore open the granola bar.

Chewing loudly, he said, "What are you doing with all that junk in your desk, anyway?"

"You never know when you might face an emergency," said Matthew.

He began taking an inventory of his kit. There were first aid supplies, a metal pot holder and can opener, more emergency food bars, and some sundry camping items like light sticks. He had a good compass, a metal cup, water purification tablets, a lighter and matches, and some emergency ponchos and space blankets. There was also a pry bar, spare batteries, and multitool. He was careful not to let Kepler put his eyes on that. Company rules forbade knives in the workplace. He did not want the blade on the multitool to get him into any trouble should Kepler speak of what he'd seen later.

He switched on the radio, tuned it to the AM band, and waited.

"...Continued unrest across the city as this latest blackout prompts frustrated citizens to lash out," said the announcer. "A county-wide advisory has been implemented urging no unnecessary travel. We have reports of rioting downtown."

"That was us, today," Kepler said. "Those animals assaulted me in broad daylight and there was nothing anyone could do!"

"...No estimate of power restoration at this time," said the radio's announcer. "With thousands of affected customers in the major metropolitan area, repair crews are stretched thin trying to see to the repairs. Authorities indicate that the problem may be worse than initially assessed because rioters are targeting power lines and deliberately cutting them."

"You see?" Kepler said. "You see? It's all falling apart. Overnight."

"Reports are now coming in of a motorcycle gang or gangs roving the city at night," said the flat voice from the radio. "This comes amidst renewed charges of arson that may or may not be linked to the motorcycle club 'The Dark Kings.'"

"It's not overnight," said Matthew, trying to distract Kepler and wondering if he should switch off the radio. "This has been boiling for weeks. The rolling blackouts. That business with the shooting last year by that neighborhood watch fellow. Racial tensions, economic tensions. The recession is worse than ever. And this heat. It's all coming to a head now, Daniel, but it's been working its way up to this for a long time. We've all seen this coming. We had to."

"This is crazy," said Kepler. His pacing increased in frequency. Blood droplets started to speck his shirt; he had gotten himself so worked up his bruised nose leaking again. "This is crazy. We're a civilization. We're better than this. How can everything we've built just come apart at the seams. How?"

" Chief of Police Joe Morris urges citizens not to panic," said the radio announcer.

The station cut to a canned sound bite of the Chief

of Police. Matthew looked up as Kepler grabbed him by the shirt.

"Everything's falling apart!" he said again. His eyes were red-rimmed and wide. "What are we going to do? What are we going to do?"

Matthew thought, just then, that he was staring into the eyes of a madman.

Chapter 3

Morning dawned hazy and thick, with humidity levels that left the back of Matthew's neck damp when he pushed himself up. The couch in the lobby wasn't particularly comfortable, but the heat had been the worst part. It wasn't the only time Matthew had spent a night in the office, although on those previous occasions, he had been pushing to finish an important presentation by deadline.

On the upholstered chair opposite him, Kepler snored loudly.

Matthew sighed. It had taken him a good two hours to talk Kepler down out of his frantic state last night. Between the two of them they had eaten the energy bars and other food items in Matthew's office kit. He had a small cache of power bars and some bottled water in his desk, but they couldn't stay at the office forever. More importantly, Matthew didn't want to stay here. He had not been able to get through to his wife all evening. His phone was an older model, which held a charge better than Kepler's high-drain smartphone, but his battery was nearing the half mark. Eventually he would need to recharge it using the external battery charger and cable he kept in his day bag. There wasn't much point in doing that, however, because both his and Kepler's phones now displayed "No Network Access" warnings. The wireless grid was down.

Matthew walked to the large plate-glass windows, where his survival radio was propped on the cross-frame for better reception. The building's steel construction meant it was hard to get a good AM signal farther into the cube farm of the second floor. While Matthew still had quite a few extra batteries for the radio, he didn't use them. He had other plans for those. Instead he flipped out the crank on the side of the little device and began turning it in even, rhythmic strokes. The dynamo inside would slowly charge the radio's internal battery, but it took quite a while to build up a charge of any duration.

He was almost done with his chore when Kepler stirred in his chair. The man ran a hand over his face and then blinked at Matthew. He jerked his chin at the radio.

"Anything?"

"It's coming in now," said Matthew.

The news was bleak. Conditions in the city had worsened overnight. The power was still off for most residents. Temperatures during the day were expected to be higher than ever. The National Guard had been called in that morning, but apparently there was some confusion about deployment, leading to chaotic and sometimes ineffective deployment of the troops. Large portions of the city were not covered by any law at all, martial or otherwise.

Some theories for the burst of violence in the last two days were being offered by the talk show hosts and news analysts. Apparently, police had responded to the first of the latest downtown riots, but in the process had killed someone. The reporter went on to describe the victim as a woman in her mid-thirties.

She had apparently died after being shot with a rubber riot-control bullet. Matt had read about the tactics used to quell civil unrest. If he remembered correctly, rubber bullets were supposed to be fired into the pavement, where they bounced and ricocheted into the crowd to make them disperse. Such rounds were dangerous tools, not harmless "stun bullets," and were supposed to be used for very serious scenarios only.

Everything he had researched about getting caught in civil unrest had taught him the same thing: You stayed away from the police in a riot. They couldn't tell you from the rest of the mob. They were likely to use force if you got close. That force could kill you despite the best intentions of the authorities. Getting struck in the head by a tear-gas grenade as it was fired, for example, would do you no favors. And then there were the rubber bullets, which could kill if used improperly. It might not even be the case that anyone had done anything wrong. People sometimes died from being tazed simply because they had medical conditions or weaknesses that the police had no way to detect.

"...maintained the No Unnecessary Travel advisory," droned local news reporter. "Local roadways continue to be jammed and Department of Transportation officials are urging citizens to remain at home. Rioting and sporadic arson fires are still flaring—"

The voice from the radio became much quieter and then stopped. Matthew picked up the unit and began cranking the dynamo again.

"What are we going to do?" Kepler asked. He sounded hopeless and afraid. Despair would kill them both quicker than anything else. Matthew could not permit that.

"We're going to walk," said Matthew. He nodded to Kepler's dress shoes. "Do you have anything besides those?"

"Besides what? My shoes? No."

"They'll have to do, then," said Matthew. He had a nicely broken-in pair of hiking boots in his cubicle, which he kept for taking lunchtime walks during cooler weather. He would change into those. Matthew went to his cubicle with Daniel trailing behind. There, he repacked the contents of his office survival kit, leaving out the canteen and web belt he kept inside.

"I still can't believe you just had that whole thing here," said Kepler.

"Here," said Matthew. He opened his desk drawer and began piling power bars on the desktop. "Take a couple of these. And find a water bottle. There's probably one in the kitchen."

"I have one at my desk."

"Good," said Matthew. "Fill it from the tap in the break room. This one too." He handed Kepler the canteen.

"What the hell is all this for?"

"We can't carry enough water for our daily needs," said Matthew. "Not really. It would be too heavy. I have chemical water purifying tablets in my bag here. And the gear we would need to boil water, which is better. We probably won't need to be out there long enough to have to find water, but you never know."

"What are you talking about?" Kepler asked.

"We're going to walk, Daniel," said Matthew. "We can't get anywhere in cars. You heard the radio. The roads are jammed."

"They said to stay put."

"You can if you want," said Matthew. "I'm walking across town. I need to make sure my family is safe. We don't have enough supplies to stay here, not without going out and foraging for more. Frankly, if I'm going to do that, I'd rather be making my way to my wife and daughter."

"But it's... we can't just walk," said Kepler. That could take, like, days."

"It's not that far," said Matthew. "But it's not close, either. Come on. Get the water. Stay or come with me if you want. Your call."

Kepler muttered something and walked away. Matthew began sorting the contents of his day bag and lengthening the shoulder strap so he could sling it over his body. He heard the faucet in the break room running, to his relief. Much as he didn't enjoy Kepler's company, the two of them had a better chance of surviving as a group than one lone traveler did. Kepler was an adult male of reasonable size and had, Matthew knew, done his share of brawling in local pubs (or so Kepler had told him). The addition of Kepler to this little expedition would hopefully make both of them a less attractive target should they run into more hostile groups — like the Hispanic street gang they'd encountered.

What worried Matthew most was simply the fact that they were downtown. It was a congested area and there was a good chance they would encounter other people. He would have preferred to avoid other citizens at all costs.

Slinging his day bag over his shoulder and across his chest, he added the survival kit to the other side.

"You look like you're wearing saddle bags," said Kepler. He had returned with the water bottle and Matthew's canteen.

"Do you have anything you can carry things in?" Matthew asked. "A duffel bag or something?"

"I've got my gym bag," said Kepler.

"Good. Bring that. Keep it light. We'll use it to accumulate anything we find along the way that might be useful, if things go wrong and we're walking longer than I think we'll be.

"Why don't we just fill it with junk from here in the office?"

"Because most of what you'll find here won't help us," said Matthew. "And if your bag is too heavy it will just slow us down. You'll notice that both of my bags are fairly light. It's important that we be able to walk without becoming fatigued or injuring a shoulder muscle or whatever."

"We could break open the vending machines downstairs, empty them out."

"That's not a bad idea," said Matthew. "But I checked last night. The machines are running low. The guy comes on Fridays to fill them. Some old corn chips and a can of soda aren't what we need to sustain us."

"You're serious about walking across town?"

"I am," said Matthew. "But there's something else I need to do first." He took the bandanna from his pocket, unfolded it on his desktop, and took a handful of spare batteries from his survival kit. Then he tied off the bandanna with the batteries inside.

"What's that for?"

Matthew swung the improvised sap through the air. He banged it against the desktop lightly. The impact reverberated through the darkened cubicle farm.

"It's a weapon," said Matthew. "One that we might need. Because we may encounter people who'll try to stop us. People who'll want to take what we have."

Kepler's eyes widened. "You're kidding."

"I'm deadly serious, Daniel. Let's go."

Chapter 4

"I thought you said we couldn't drive anywhere," said Kepler. He was carrying a plastic grocery bag in which rode two bottles of water and three bags of corn chips. Over his shoulder he had slung his gym bag.

"We can't," said Matt. "We'll get snarled in traffic like before and go nowhere."

"Why is it so hot?" Kepler demanded. He ran his fingers through his scalp and blew air through clenched teeth. "Are you sure about this?"

"You can stay here if you want," said Matt. "Or walk home. You're welcome to come with me, but you don't have to."

"No," said Kepler. "No, I'll go with you." Fear crossed his face, then, and Matt knew he would be thinking about their encounter with the gang on the ramp. There was a lot of territory to cover between the office and ... anywhere else, really. A good chunk of that was downtown, which Matt wasn't looking forward to traversing. Having someone to watch his back, even someone like Kepler, had its appeal. Kepler would be thinking much the same thing.

"I need my kit from the car," Matt explained. "And we should take at least one of the floormats."

"Floormats? What for?"

Matt waved him off. He went to his Toyota Camry in the office parking lot, which was looking fairly deserted. As he approached the car he realized something wasn't right. It took him a moment to figure out that his antenna had been bent at an odd angle. Looking around the vehicle, he was relieved to see none of the tires had been flattened.

"You had better get out of here, you two," said a voice.

Matthew recognized him. It was Steven Mercer, the day-shift security guard for the office. He had removed his uniform shirt, stripping down to his striped pants and t-shirt. Matt watched him ball up the uniform shirt and toss it into the nearby dumpster.

"Steven?" Matthew asked. "What are you doing?"

"I'm getting the hell out of here," he said. "This place can burn to the ground for all I care."

"But..." Matthew said. "Shouldn't someone guard the building?"

"I've been listening to the CB in my car," said Mercer. "They're beating up anybody in uniform they can find alone. And there's racial violence, too. White people getting beaten for being white, that kind of thing. The balloon has gone up, Matt. It's the end of the world as we know it."

"I don't believe that," said Matthew. "This will pass."

"They're going to come through here like locusts," said Mercer. "Mobs. Violent mobs. And if you're the wrong color or the wrong flavor or whatever, they're going to kill you. Get out of the city, Matthew. I'm going to my cabin at Cranberry Lake. If you're smart, you'll get out. Before somebody kills you."

Mercer got into his pickup truck and drove off. Kepler ran up to stand next to Matthew. "Was that Steve Mercer?"

"Yeah," said Matthew.

"What did he say?"

"Nothing," said Matthew. "Nothing."

"Aww, man," Kepler said, noticing the vandalism to Matt's car. His voice was shrill, almost a whine. "Those dirty sons of—"

"It can't be helped," said Matt. "Better check yours."

The idea that his own precious BMW might have been vandalized seemed to get Kepler's attention. He hurried over to where his own car was parked, walked a circle around it, and threw Matt a thumbs-up.

"We'd better move them," said Matt. "Let's put them as far out of sight as we can. They're targets in the middle of a mostly empty lot."

"But where?" Kepler asked as Matt walked over to speak without shouting.

Matt surveyed the lot. He shook his head. "It's not much," he said, "but let's park them over there, near the dumpster. In the lee of the building. At least then they're not just sticking out like sore thumbs here."

They moved their respective vehicles. Matt paused to take the canvas shoulder bag out of the trunk of the Camry. The bag was of olive drab canvas, distressed to lighten its color. It was as nondescript as anything someone could carry.

"That looks like a college student's messenger bag," said Kepler. "Or a... you know. A messenger's messenger bag."

"That's the idea," said Matt. He rifled through the bag for a moment, then tested the power tool bag on his shoulder. "I should have thought of that," he said finally. "The tool bag will hurt after I carry it for a while. That's no good." He began sorting the contents of both the canvas bag and the tool bag, mixing and matching, throwing the items he wanted to keep in the messenger sack.

"What is all that?" asked Kepler.

"My car survival kit," said Matt. "Some of the stuff in here is just for the car. Jumper cables, that kind of thing. I'd like to keep them but it's too much weight, especially since we'll be on foot. It would be nice to know we could jump start a car we came across, but I can't afford to carry anything I can't use." He looked at the gym bag on Kepler's shoulder. "Does that thing have a shoulder strap?" he asked.

Kepler had been wearing the bag over his shoulder using the side handles. "Yeah," he said. "I can zip it out of the pouch."

"Do that, then," Matt said. "We want to be hands free if we can. "But don't put the water and other stuff in it. It will be too heavy. Tie that to your belt on the opposite side using the handles of the plastic bag."

"You're pushy. You know that, Avery?"

Matt shrugged. "It's just a suggestion."

"Survival bags in the office. Survival bags in the car. I suppose you've got a survival bag at home, too, and probably one stashed at grandma's house over the river and through the woods."

Matt shrugged. "Some people golf."

"But you prepare," Kepler said. "I get it."

Matt reached into his car and took one of the floormats. He handed it to Kepler. "Here," he said. "You carry that."

"What the hell for?" asked Kepler.

"We've got to cross behind the bank to get to Second," Matt explained. "Then I guess, down past the Federal Building. I'd rather not get that deep into the middle of downtown, but I don't know of a better route. The only other option would be the bridge after Elm, and I don't want to get trapped on a bridge if we can help it."

"What difference does that make?" Kepler asked. He hurried to keep up, slinging the floormat over his shoulder, as Matt set a brisk pace. Around them, they could hear the sounds of cars honking, people yelling, and once, what sounded like a trio of car-mufflers backfiring. Matt tried to tell himself that was all it was. He was not convinced.

"We're traveling overland by foot," Matt explained. "We're a limited party, although two is better than one alone. We need to be able to avoid trouble where we encounter it. A bridge, a tunnel, any narrow route, is a natural choke point. Choke points can be useful — remember that movie with all the CGI, about the Spartan warriors?"

"This... Is... Spa—" Kepler started to yell.

"Don't yell," Matt interrupted. "Yeah, that one. It's based on a real event. A small force of Spartan warriors, horribly outnumbered, used a natural choke point to hold off a much larger army. The narrow point of travel eliminates the advantage of numbers."

"Then why don't we want that?"

"Well, for one, those 300 Spartans all died," said Matt. "For another, we're not fighting a war. We want to avoid trouble, and if we get caught in a narrow pass, it stops us from going around a problem. Our only choices would be to advance into it or retreat from it. Whenever you run, Daniel, you can't afford to do it in a straight line. Whoever's chasing you can run you right over."

"Well what does any of that have to do with me carrying a frigging floormat on my back?"

Matt stopped. They had reached the first obstacle, but he had planned for this. He pointed. "That," he said.

The chain link fence behind the bank building had been erected to stop homeless people from camping out among the dumpsters behind the bank, where a set of alleys was formed by the structure and its closest neighbors. On top of the fence was a triple string of barbed wire.

"What are we doing?" Kepler asked.

Matt flipped the floormat over the fence and on top of the barbed wire strands, creating a narrow aisle of safe passage. The heavy synthetic rubber of the matt prevented the barbs from penetrating. Matt threw his bags over the fence and gestured for Kepler to do the same. Then he hoisted himself up and landed, if a bit heavily, on the other side.

"Come on," said Matt. He gestured. "Up and over, Daniel."

"What's that noise?" Kepler asked, looking through the fence and past where Matt stood. The mouth of the alley beyond echoed with shouts and the sounds of glass breaking.

Matt turned. "Hurry!" he said. "Now, Daniel. Go now! Come on!"

"But what—"

"No time!" Matt insisted.

Just then, the leading edge of the angry mob drew even with the mouth of the alley.

Chapter 5

Matt helped Kepler down from the fence. He threw the man's bags to him and shouldered his own. Then he gestured for a piece of metal pipe jutting from one of the dumpsters. "Grab that!" he yelled. He snatched up a piece of wood that might have once been part of a cargo pallet. It was half the width of a two-by-four and as long as his arm.

"You can't mean to fight a mob?" Kepler said, turning paler.

"No," said Matt. "Just be quiet, Daniel. Stay close behind me. Don't let yourself be separated from me, not for any reason. And whatever you do, don't fall down. You might get trampled. Now do what I do!"

Matt pressed himself against the alley and shuffled down the wall, on the side opposite the direction of the mob's travel. He slid along the wall until he was very near the opening to the street beyond. The noise of the mob was almost deafening; shouts echoed down the alleyway and crashed against his ears. He ignored that, instead focused solely on his goal, pausing only long enough to jerk his chin toward the alley mouth so Daniel would follow.

When he judged he was close enough, he raised his wooden club high over his head... and stepped out into the crowd.

"Yeah!" he shouted, pumping the club in the air. There were other members of the mob with weapons. The nearest of them glanced at Matt and nodded their approval. Matt mustered up his best expression of total outrage and, careful to keep his eyes ahead of the mob as if fixed on some distant enemy, some faraway target of his anger, he did his best to imitate the other mobgoers.

"What's in the bag, man?" shouted the man to his left. He was dressed in a t-shirt and shorts and had another t-shirt tied over his face and head like a ninja's mask. "What you got?"

"Buncha stuff from there," Matt pointed vaguely behind himself, over the heads of the crowd. "It's like Christmas!"

"Yeah!" grinned the man. "Christmas! Right on, dude. Right on."

Behind Matt, Kepler was also imitating the marching rioters. Egged on by some of the mobgoers around him, he took his pipe and smashed out the side window of a dented US Mail truck parked on the street in front of the

Federal Building. The truck had already been spray-painted and bore numerous dents and key-marks. Slogans of some kind had been scratched into its paint, but Matt could not read them. He slowed his pace as much as he dared, hoping Kepler would tire of his role-playing and catch up. The two were almost out of sight of each other when Kepler finally tired of his vandalism and hurried on.

The next part would take carefully maneuvering. As casually as he could, Matt worked his way through the crowd, crossing from the West to the East side of the street as he slowly threaded his way amongst the mob. Kepler, fortunately, saw what he was doing and realized the significance of Matt's slow change of position. The two were close enough to each other for Matt's plan to work when the next break between buildings occurred.

Do what I do, Matt thought. Just follow me, Daniel.

As he reached the gap between the structures, he simply turned hard right and walked casually down the alley, still pumping his wooden club above his head. Kepler did the same. The two men drew abreast of each other near the end of the alleyway.

"I can't believe you... pulled that off," said Kepler, breathing hard. His face was flushed.

"You didn't have to get quite so into it," Matt said. "What if you're on camera smashing that mail truck?"

"Oh, come off it, Matt," Kepler said. "How many hundreds of people you think are out there?" he pointed his thumb back over his shoulder. The noise of the mob was still very loud. "You think the cops are going to arrest one or two people when ten times that are doing things they shouldn't?"

"What do you suppose they were rioting about?" Matt asked.

"Who cares?" Kepler said. "You know as well as I do, Matt, it's been hot for, like, ever. If anybody's to blame for the blackouts, it's probably the folks in charge. I know it sure as hell isn't you or me."

"Yeah," Matt said. He hoped his voice did not carry the doubt he felt. He had not anticipated a full-blown riot, not so soon after the latest outage. He should have. Had he been thinking he would have planned an alternate route that gave the Federal Building, and the rest of downtown, a wider berth.

"HEY!" shouted a voice that echoed through the alley. "What are you doing there?"

Kepler turned. Holding his pipe like a baseball bat, he took a step forward.

The kid at the end of the alley had broken away from the mob. He had what looked like a handkerchief wrapped around his fist. When he saw Kepler and Matt, he began charging down the alleyway.

"Wait," said Matt.

"I got this," said Kepler.

"No—" Matt had time to say.

Kepler swung the pipe. He hit the boy — who looked about the right age to be a college student — alongside the jaw. There was a sickening crack. The kid crumpled in a heap, his limbs suddenly rubber. Kepler dropped as if he meant to check the kid.

"He may be hurt badly," said Matt. It was then that he realized that Kepler wasn't checking the boy's pulse or breathing. He was going through his pockets. "Daniel, what the hell are you doing?"

Kepler looked up. "He's alive," he said, sounding defensive. "He was coming at us. He was going to attack us. He could tell we weren't with the rioters."

"You don't know that."

"Yeah?" Kepler grabbed the unconscious kid's arm and held up the boy's right hand. "Then you tell me, Matt, since you know all about this stuff. What's going on with this?"

The boy's right hand was thick with electrical tape over the knuckles. The wad of tape was heavy and thick, covering the area the kid would have used to punch if he balled his hand into a fist. Kepler began pulling tape free, unwinding it as quickly as he could.

"What are you doing?" Matt asked again. "We need to go."

Something heavy fell out of the wad of tape and rang on the pavement of the alley. Matt looked nervously back the way they had come, anxious to get farther away lest other rioters see what they were doing.

"We used to do this in high school," said Kepler. "I grew up in Brooklyn, remember?" He held up the object that had fallen out of the tape wrapping and then tossed it to Matt. "It's a pewter chess piece, Matt. Heavy as hell. The kid wrapped up his hand to make himself some homemade brass knuckles. He was going to knock my jaw clean off my face."

"We should call an ambulance," Matt said. He stared at the chess piece and then put it in his pocket.

"How?" Kepler asked. "And who cares what happens to this punk?"

The boy began to stir. "H...hey..." he started to say. "Help. Help!"

"Come on," urged Matt. "They're going to hear him."

"Sure," said Kepler. "Now you want to go. At least he's alive."

"HELP!" shouted the boy.

"GO!" Matt ordered Kepler.

They ran. Matt didn't like it. Kepler was too quick to decide the rules were null and void. But if they stayed, they risked being torn apart by the mob.

Behind him, Matt could see the orange flicker of deliberately set fires.

Chapter 6

The wail of sirens and the sounds of distant gunfire punctuated the long walk across town. After the near-miss with the mob downtown, Matt had directed them through a number of narrow side streets, avoiding larger thoroughfares whenever possible. He did not want to be caught in the open if he could help it.

They walked in silence for many hours. Twice, police cars sped past them, and once a fire truck with its lights and sirens going. Matt was not certain, but he thought he saw bullet holes in the cracked glass of the side windows of the fire truck. Was the city really so out of control? Were his fellow citizens so quick to go from the veneer of civilization to complete chaos? It seemed so. He had worried about it for years — ever since the stories of rape, looting, and other civil unrest in the wake of Hurricane Katrina had prompted him to turn to survivalism, to "prepping." But until now he had never truly believed it could take so little to set his city to destroying itself.

Matt stuck his hands in his pockets. He had the homemade sap, his bandanna full of batteries. He had practiced with the improvised weapon on a torso-shaped rubber dummy, his "Body Opponent Bag." He had also used it to bash apart old junk behind his house, like the rickety old kitchen chair his wife had finally given him permission to throw away. But he had never had to use such a weapon on a human being. If the kid had come at him instead of Kepler, would he have had the guts to use it? Would he have spotted the taped-up knuckle duster that Kepler recognized from his childhood?

"So what was that deal back by the Federal Building?" Kepler finally asked. "For a minute there I thought you weren't so uptight." Kepler was using the iron pipe for a walking stick. He had not been able to keep his hands off the thing since getting a taste of the power it offered him.

Matt sighed. He supposed he could not stop talking to Kepler altogether, not if he needed the man's backup. "When I realized we were walking into a mob," he explained, "we had two choices. We could go back the way we came, put the barbed-wire fence between us and them. That would have worked in the short term, but it would have cut us off from our goal. And if they had decided to come after us, there were enough people in that crowd to push the fence over if they really tried."

"Like a zombie movie," said Kepler. A look of sudden

recognition crossed his face. "Wait," he said. "That's what we did with the mob, isn't it? We pretended to be zombies so the others wouldn't recognize us."

"That's exactly what we did," Matt nodded. "Your best bet, if you're caught in a mob, is to pretend to be part of it. Play along. Make the rest of the mob think you're just one of them. Then you work your way at right angles to get away from it when you can. We did something risky by moving into the middle of the crowd, but it was necessary to get to the other side of the street. Whenever possible you want to stay to the outer perimeter of a mass of people like that. Better options for movement, and less chance you'll get trampled."

"You talk like they're not people anymore," said Kepler. "Those were just people fed up with how bad it's gotten. It felt good to smash that truck."

"Zombies, remember?" Matt said. "A mob moves like water. You have to use a building or some other obstacle, get into the lee of it so you're not caught in the tidal surge. That's why I broke for the alley to get away. And of course we needed to get past them to keep going home."

"What if there hadn't been an alley?"

"Then I would have chosen a building that looked unlocked, walked in through the front door, and found our way out through the back door. But that's more risky because a locked door can stop you."

"You don't have something in your Indiana Jones bag for door locks?" Kepler asked.

"I have a small prybar," Matt admitted. "Good for most locks. Maybe not a really heavy padlock or something, but for most locked doors, you don't have to fight the lock itself. You just have to break the doorjamb around the lock." He did not add that the prybar, too, could serve as a weapon, if needed. It was a potent stabbing implement.

"Where did you learn all this stuff?" Kepler asked.

"There are a lot of training programs available, if you just look," said Kepler. "The Internet is a great resource. If you know what to look for."

Kepler snorted. "And to think I've been using it to look for naked chicks all this time."

Matt ignored that. It was just one more block until home. The neighborhood they were in was, technically, outside the city limits, although the area was much more dense than one would typically consider a "suburb." It was part of the "urban sprawl" that so many people talked about these days — the blurring of the line between the city proper and its outlying areas. Matt had talked with his wife, Jennifer, many times about packing up and moving out of the city, getting clear of the worst of it and living someplace safely rural. She thought the idea was crazy. She had no intention of living "miles from everything," as she put it.

"There," Matt said, when finally his house was in view. "There it is."

"Vinyl siding?" Kepler asked. "Good call."

Matt looked at him. After a moment, he said, "Come

on. Let's get inside."

As they approached, Matt took in the damage to the neighborhood. He listened for the hum of a generator, but did not hear one — not his own, which his wife should have switched on, and not the Schilling's down the street. That didn't worry him too much; he had warned Jennifer not to run the generator all day if it could be helped, especially if the street outside was still and quiet.

There was litter strewn across the street. The contents of several trash cans had been emptied into the middle of the quiet side road, and he saw at least three smashed mailboxes. Someone had come through with a baseball bat or some other weapon, smashing the boxes on their poles at the end of his neighbors' driveways. He was relieved to see that his own mailbox had been missed. Across the street, the Lewis house had lost its bay windows to bricks or rocks. Next door to his house, what looked like a small fire had burned a black circle into the steps of the Miller house.

Probably a flaming bag of dog crap, Matt thought. Little vandals are lucky they didn't burn down the entire house.

When he reached his own driveway, he realized what was bothering him: Jennifer's Hyundai hatchback was not in the driveway. It was possible she had moved it to the portable carport behind the house, which he used to keep firewood dry. He had mentioned that to her once, but was surprised she had listened. Then he realized it was just as likely the car had been stolen from the driveway.

His house had not escaped the passing vandals unscathed. Profane graffiti had been spray-painted in large, black letters across the front of his garage, and two of the garage windowpanes had been shattered. He paused long enough to look through one of these and saw that his Subaru wagon was still inside. It appeared unharmed.

Kepler followed as Matt took out his keys and unlocked the front door. He was displeased to see the deadbolt was not thrown. He had asked his wife to use it daily, but she rarely did when he was out.

"Jen, I'm here," he called out as the door opened. "I brought Daniel from the office with me."

"Hello?" Kepler called.

The house was completely still. Matt checked the kitchen, the master bedroom, and even the basement. Then he thought to check the bathroom, which he had told his family would be the "safe room" in case of emergencies. There was a phone extension in there and the door was reinforced. There was no one in the bathroom, either.

Matt's family was gone.

Chapter 7

"Your shoe," Kepler said, pointing.

Matt looked down. Stuck to the heel of his shoe was a post-it note. As Kepler sank gratefully into the couch in the living room, complaining about how much his feet hurt after their marathon trek from downtown, Matt read and then reread the note. Apparently it had been on the front door, then fallen to the step, where he had walked on it while entering the house.

"Don't feel safe here," the note read. "Don't know when you'll get this. Gone to Carol's. Melissa says to tell Daddy hello." It was signed with a hand-drawn heart and Jennifer's name.

Carol was Jennifer's sister. She didn't live far away by car, but the distance would feel considerably magnified by conditions on the streets. Then, too, there was the fact that a No Unnecessary Travel order was in effect. Matt forced himself not to swear aloud. He did not want Kepler to know how frustrated he felt.

"What are you going to do?" Kepler asked.

"I'm going to her sister's to get her," said Matt. "Carol has a place in the city. It's no safer than where we are, and probably less. I can't just sit here while they're out there, unprotected." He hefted his shoulder bag. The supplies he had with him would be adequate for the trip to Carol's and back, or should be. He did not want to open the safe room stores with Kepler nearby. He could not quite bring himself to trust his coworker. Kepler's violent streak worried him. He would have to make an exception when it came to personal protection, however. "I'll be right back," Matt said.

He went into his bedroom and slid the locking cabinet out from under the bed. Using a key from his key ring, he opened the cabinet and removed from it what looked like a long-barreled revolver with a shoulder stock. The carbine had a light mounted beneath its barrel and a simple 1X-power red-dot scope mounted on top of the frame. He took a box of .45 Long Colt shells and a box of .410 shotgun shells from the cabinet, replaced the case under the bed, and brought the weapon out into the living room.

"Whoa," said Kepler. "What you got there, Rambo?"

"It's called the Circuit Judge," said Matt. "Jen doesn't like guns. Never has. She refused to let me keep a handgun in the house."

"She keep your balls in her purse, too?"

Matt had nothing to say to that. He hefted the weapon, opened the cylinder, and began to load it with the .45 Long Colt ammunition. "It can fire shotgun shells or these rounds. The rifle was Jen's concession to my wish to have a gun. It gives me the versatility of a revolver and the reach of a carbine. The shotgun loads are good for hunting."

"I'll let you know if I see any bears," Kepler cracked. "Why not use the shotgun shells for home defense? Isn't that what people do? Keep the buckshot from going through walls and such?"

"Unfortunately, it doesn't work that way," said Matt. He finished loading the weapon and was careful to hold it across his chest with the barrel pointing toward the floor. "Most loads, even shotgun pellets, will go through drywall. Most bullets will pass right through an interior wall and a lot of them will go through the exterior of the house. I don't use the shotgun loads for defense because you never know where your pattern is going to spread to, not exactly. You can't afford to hit an innocent person. Might as well be a fire hose, beyond a certain distance."

"Whatever you say, Dirty Harry. We leaving?"

"If you want to come with me," said Matt. He debated offering to let Kepler stay behind to guard the house, but wasn't sure he trusted the man enough. Kepler might take it on himself to search through the home looking for supplies. Besides, his original reason for wanting Kepler along, as backup, still held.

"Now that you're packing heat, you bet I'm coming

with you," said Kepler. "You don't have a spare one of those you can give me?"

"No," said Matt. "Wish I did." That wasn't strictly true. He would not have given Kepler a gun if he had the choice. The man held his metal pipe in the crook of his arm as if it were his most prized possession.

Matt secured the front door as best he could, using the dead bolt and drawing all of the curtains. He wished he had time to secure the windows with the plywood he kept in the garage, but that was a job that would take some time. He wanted to go now and get to Jennifer and Melissa, make sure they were where he could keep them safe.

He was also furious that she hadn't listened to him. They had not talked about it as much as he would have liked, because Jennifer did not share his enthusiasm for "prepping," but they had discussed it. Their emergency plan, should something happen while Matt was at work, was for Jennifer and Melissa to stay at the house and wait for him to return. Once reunited, they would make plans for wherever else they might have to "bug out" to. Barring an extreme emergency that forced Jennifer to evacuate the house, she should have been here waiting.

Don't feel safe here. The words echoed in his mind. He could not fault her for taking her car and leaving if conditions were too dangerous to permit them to stay. She had access to the gun; she had a copy of the same key. But Matthew would bet she had buried the key in the jewelry cabinet on top of her dresser and had not touched it since he gave it to her. She hated guns and had barely tolerated him showing her how to load, unload, and operate the Circuit Judge carbine. Even getting her that far had been a major accomplishment for Matthew, as they had argued for months about buying the weapon beforehand.

Matthew checked the SureFire flashlight in the rail mount under the barrel. It was nice and bright. He pointed. "Through the kitchen," he said. "The car's in the garage."

Locking the door to the kitchen behind them, Matthew paused long enough to grab the two extra gas cans he kept next to the lawnmower. Grabbing bungee cords off the pegboard in the garage, he began to strap the cans to the roof rack of his Subaru wagon.

"What's that all about?" Kepler asked.

"We have no idea if gas stations will be open," said Matt. "Or if we'll dare stop for fuel. I'm going to cover the cans with a tarp so no one can tell what's up here. No need to tempt thieves. The longer the power is out, the more people will want gas for their cars and generators, if they have them."

"You could just put them in the back and cover them up," Kepler said.

"The fumes would drive us out of the car eventually," said Matt. There was a set of portable chairs, the kind that collapsed to be worn in Nylon travel sacks over the shoulder, in one corner of the garage. Matt picked up one of these and began removing the chair from its bag.

Kepler made a face. "Okay, now I'm really confused,

Rambo. What's the lawn chair for?"

"Not the chair," said Matt. "The bag." He put the Circuit Judge in the chair sack and pulled the drawstring. "Now if we have to carry the rifle it won't look like a weapon."

"Not bad," said Kepler. He slid into the passenger seat as Matt climbed into the driver's side, placing the disguised rifle on the back seat behind them. "I'm surprised you don't have a Jeep or something."

"The Subaru has all-wheel drive and gets better mileage," said Matt. "Besides, it doesn't attract as much attention as a big four-wheel drive. And I'll take a well-maintained family car over a macho off-road vehicle any day." He pushed the automatic garage door opener without thinking. Nothing happened.

"I'll get it," said Kepler. The man climbed out, opened the garage door, and waited for Matt to pull out. Then he closed the door behind them and turned the handle to the "lock" position before piling back in.

As the Subaru pulled out of the driveway, neither man saw the figures approaching the house from the opposite end of the street.

Chapter 8

The bottle that struck the windshield shattered, leaving a crack in the auto's glass and covering the front of the Subaru in beer.

"Hold on!" Matt shouted. He threw the wagon into reverse and stepped on the gas. The Subaru flew backward, dodging trash cans, broken wooden pallets, and other debris in the road.

Matt had tried to plan the route to Carol's house with an eye toward avoiding population areas. Unfortunately, his primary and secondary routes had been blocked by police cars enforcing the No Unnecessary Travel order. They had spotted these — with Kepler using the pair of binoculars Matt had given him from Matt's survival gear — far enough off to back up and take a different street, but the result was that they had come uncomfortably close to downtown once more. There they had encountered the mob once more as the mass of rioters rounded a corner and nearly swamped them.

"You should turn around," said Kepler. "Put it in four-wheel-drive or whatever and just run them down! They're trying to kill us!"

Matt spared him an angry glare and spun the wheel, bringing the car around so he could point the nose away from the mob. More bottles and rocks hit the rear of the wagon. The rear window shattered. Matt put the pedal to the floor, sending the Subaru speeding down the street. He was forced to dodge an overturned cop car and a burned-out panel van as he did so.

"We don't stand a chance against a mob," said Matt. "Have you thought about what could happen if you drive into a crowd like that? We'd kill a few, sure. We'd injure many more. And then the crush of bodies would be so great they'd start rocking the vehicle until they tipped us over, dragged us out, and beat us to death. It's happened before. People think their cars make them invulnerable. Nothing is more powerful than hundreds of angry people."

Something whined off the roof of the Subaru. The metallic noise was joined by another, then a third.

"They're shooting as us!" screamed Kepler. Somebody's shooting at us!" He was forced to hang onto his passenger strap as Matt took a sharp corner, very nearly putting the Subaru up on two wheels. Then he tried to reach back for the Circuit Judge on the back seat. "I'll aim out the window and shoot back!"

"No!" Matt shouted. He pushed Kepler's arm away from the rifle. Kepler turned red. His eyes blazed. Matt was insistent. "We are not taking pot shots at random people! You don't even know who's firing, or where they're shooting from. They could be in any of a dozen buildings all around us. It could be a thrill-sniper, on a roof somewhere, and we'd never spot him. You don't challenge odds like those. You get the hell out! And you sure don't murder innocent people. Don't touch that gun again."

Kepler opened his mouth as if to say something. Then he turned sharply away. He stared out the window for the remainder of the trip across town.

They had been forced to detour around a police roadblock yet again by the time they finally pulled into Carol's driveway. Twilight was giving way to darkness. It was at times like these, when the streetlights did not work, that Matt realized just how dark the night could be. Even in the middle of the night, there was always ambient light from some artificial source, either from the street lamps or porch lights on other houses. Now, with all of that out and no cars moving on the street, he barely see his own hand in front of his face. His fingers brushed the reassuring barrel of the tactical flashlight in his pocket.

He was relieved to see Jennifer's Hyundai in the driveway. His relief turned to a ball of lead in his stomach, however, as he came closer. Once he was close enough to touch the car, he could see that both rear tires of the Hyundai were flat. The rear brake lights had been smashed out.

Carol's neighborhood was still within the city limits. Houses were closer together here, and of a design with high, peaked roofs and large wraparound front porches. At least one car parked three houses down had been burned. Several of the houses had broken windows. Carol's living room picture window had been boarded up with pieces of scrap lumber.

"Hey, man," said Kepler. "Sorry I got a little out of hand there. I got your back." His face was still somewhat flushed, but he seemed sincere enough.

"It's all right," Matt told him. "Just keep an eye out behind us." He reached into the back seat, took the rifle, and pulled it free from its bag. Stuffing the chair bag in his back pocket as he climbed out of the Subaru, he held the weapon low but ready as he approached the house. He had parked his car as far up the driveway, and to the side of the Hyundai, as he could. Hopefully the smaller vehicle would at least partly screen the Subaru from the road, making it a less tempting target.

The silence on the rest of the street was eerie. In the distance, the now constant sound of civil unrest seemed almost dreamlike. How many fires could there be, that they were still hearing fire trucks? And why was there so much random gunfire? He paused for a moment and heard two more distant cracks. The sound was not the deep thunder of shotguns. He had grown up in the country, not far from a skeet- and trap-shooting range. He knew that sound.

This was higher-pitched, sharper, more ominous. It was pistol- and rifle-fire.

He wished he had an assault rifle.

The handful of rounds his Circuit Judge held seemed woefully inadequate, but for all that he was incredibly grateful to have the carbine.

He rapped on the door.

"Carol? It's Matthew. Mathew Avery. Are my wife and daughter there with you?"

There was, for a moment, not a sound from within the house. Matthew's heart leapt into his throat. Could something have happened? Were they hurt, or worse? Had his wife, his daughter, and Carol been forced to flee this house as well?

A chain rattled inside. Matt waited anxiously as the door finally opened.

His wife stood at the door.

"Jen!" Matt said, smiling. He almost forgot the gun in his hands. Jennifer made a face but let him hug her while holding the rifle to the side. Little Melissa, with all the solemnity a five-year-old could muster, looked up at them both, then at Kepler standing in the doorway.

"Daddy?" she asked. "Why do you have a gun too? Who's that man?"

The sound of a pump-action shotgun being racked almost drove Matt to the carpeted floor. He turned to see Carol leveling a Mossberg 12-gauge at the doorway.

"Matt, get down! Someone followed you!"

"Wait, no, no," said Matt. "That's Daniel Kepler. He's with me! We work together."

"Yeah, don't shoot, beautiful," said Kepler. He looked Carol up and down. She wore tight-fitting jeans and a summer-weight blouse that did nice things for her figure. Even Matt had to admit that; Carol was Jennifer's older sister, but the two were both exceptionally attractive. While Jennifer was a natural blonde, Carol's hair was auburn, which Jennifer had once sworn to him, after half a bottle of wine at the family reunion cook-out, was a dye-job.

"Quick!" said Carol. She brushed past Kepler and slammed the door shut. "Before one of them gets it into his head to try for the door!" As Matt watched, Carol replaced the door chain and took a wooden doorstop from the floor. She wedged the doorstop into the jamb to make the door harder to open.

"What's going on?" Kepler asked.

"I'm glad you're here," said Jen. Now that Matt could look at her closely, in the light from the LED lantern sitting on a nearby coffee table, he could see she looked drawn and worried. "Carol suggested we come over before the phones went dead—"

"Wait," said Kepler. "You talking about the cell phones?"

"No," said Carol. "She means the landlines. We were talking on the phone because those still worked, even with the power out. But they went dead not long after she got here. And then they started coming through the neighborhood. Breaking into houses. Setting fire to cars."

"They?" asked Kepler.

"Looters," said Carol.

Chapter 9

"Too bad we don't have any ice," said Kepler, sipping from the glass of Canadian whiskey. In the light from Carol's lantern, his eyes were hollowed by shadow. He sat on one end of the couch, trying not to look obvious as he stared at Carol's legs. She had changed into shorts as the night got later and was trying very hard not to notice Kepler's leering. Jen, meanwhile, was asleep in the guest bedroom with Melissa curled up next to her.

Sitting in a kitchen chair he had placed by the boarded-up window in the living room, Matt listened to them talk. He was watching the street through a gap in the scrap wood, trying to tell himself he did not feel nervous and afraid. His revolving carbine was resting across his legs.

"I don't like to run the generator at night," said Carol. She sipped from her own drink, although Matt had watched carefully. She was still nursing her first whiskey-and-water, while Kepler was on his third. "Makes it hard to keep the freezer... freezing."

Kepler laughed at the joke, too loudly. He stage-whispered an apology to Matt, who had twice asked him not to make so much noise. It wasn't that he wanted to prevent Jennifer and Melissa from waking up, although that was part of it. He was trying to listen to sounds from the neighborhood.

Looters had made circuits through the neighborhood twice — once right after Matt and Kepler had arrived, and once more an hour later. It was these roving bands of vandals, who were out enjoying the freedom that they could do whatever they wanted and suffer no consequences, who had damaged Jennifer's car and prompted Carol to board up the windows.

The second time the looters came, Carol had actually taken a shot at one of them through the door. At least, that was what it had looked like to Matt. She had explained later that she had aimed for the pavement short of her target, not sure she could really bring herself to kill anyone.

It was a dangerous game to play, and Matt had told her as much. You couldn't afford to play games with firearms. If you were legally justified in pointing a gun at someone, it was because you were legally justified in killing them. Warning shots were the sort of thing that could get you sued into poverty, or sent to jail, once things got back to normal.

Matt prayed things got back to normal.

It was only then, when he saw how on edge Carol was, that he had realized just how difficult all this was, for all of them. He had ignored the fear, ignored the adrenaline, because he was desperate to get to Jennifer and Melissa. But now, as he sat here watching for more of his neighbors, more of his fellow citizens, who just might want to rape his wife and sister or murder him, he could not help but feel his hands shake. His chest was tight and he knew the stress was eating away at him. He would have to make an effort to stay calm, keep his wits about him. His family needed him.

It was Carol, in fact, who had gotten him into "prepping" in the first place. She read survival magazines and liked guns. She even studied at a Karate school at the mall and was close to earning her black belt. But though her mindset was in the right place, for Carol most of survival was largely theory. While Matt had followed what he thought was her example, becoming a part-time survivalist and spending his "hobby" time working on preparing to keep his family safe, Carol had not gone farther than reading about the subject on the Internet.

He had learned that when she admitted to him that she had enough food in the house for perhaps a day more, with five of them sheltering there. She had always meant to get around to stockpiling, but short of the shotgun and a few extra boxes of shells, an emergency radio and some batteries, and a top-of-the-line first-aid kit in her car, she had almost no supplies. What little she had put away had been depleted during the time Jen and Melissa had stayed there.

It made Matt feel better to know that Carol and her shotgun had been here to protect his wife and daughter... but it was still thanks to Jen's refusal to follow their emergency plan that they were here, trapped inside someone else's house, worrying about violent looters breaking in.

Home invasion, he thought. You never think it can happen to you. It's always 'never happened before' until it happens the first time.

Despite the stress, despite the anxiety he felt over the world crashing down around him, despite his concern for his wife and daughter, he felt his eyes growing heavy. It would be so easy to just lean back in the chair a little, put his chin on his chest, let sleep... take him...

"Get your hands off me!" Carol shouted.

Matt's eyes snapped open just in time to see Carol twist Kepler's wrist in some kind of lock that made the other man yelp in pain. He withdrew his hand as if stung and jumped up from the couch, spitting obscenities at Carol.

"Hey!" Matt said.

"What? What?" Kepler demanded. "This slut practically throws herself at me and then makes with the Kung Fu when I dare to try and take her up on her offer!"

"This is my house," she said. "Don't you dare talk to me like that. You get out. You get out right now. You're not welcome here."

Matt put his gun on the chair as he stood. He put

himself between the two of them.

"Both of you, please, stop," Matt said. "We're all on edge. There's no need for—"

Kepler was suddenly in his face, grabbing Matt by his shirt. "I think I've had enough of you bossing me around," Kepler said. His voice was thick and smelled of whiskey. "You're the guy with all the answers, huh? What makes you so special, little man? You talk your way out of an ass-kicking by some barrio punks and you think that makes you the big man around here?"

Kepler hauled back his arm to punch him in the face—

Orange light leapt from the picture window, behind the boards. The crash, the almost overwhelming smell of gas, and the sudden heat hit Matt in the face. He and Kepler fell to the floor. Carol screamed.

"The gun! Carol, the gun!" Matt shouted.

"Fire extinguisher!" Carol yelled back, shaking her head. She ran from the living room, headed for the kitchen.

The rumble of motorcycle engines outside shook what was left of the glass in the pane behind the scrap wood. Matt crawled to the window and grabbed his carbine. He reached up and, with his hands, pulled free the top-most piece of wood, which was held in place with small roofing nails.

The board was on fire.

He dropped it to the floor and immediately realized his mistake. The carpet began to catch as the burning wood struck it. He stamped at it with his feet. A stinging above his cheek made him flinch, and it took him a moment to realize he had been struck with splinters of wood. Then he realized why his ears hurt, too.

Gunfire! They were shooting!

He didn't think. He raised the gun to his shoulder and, through the flames, pointed it at the nearest motorcycle. The man who rode it was visible in the reflected light from the fire at the front of the house. He was holding a pistol of some kind in his hand. He saw Matt and leveled the gun at him...

Matt fired.

The biker returned fire. Bullets punched holes through Matt's flimsy cover, pocking the walls and ceiling behind and above him.

Squeeze the trigger, he told himself. Aim and squeeze. If they kill you, they kill you. Drop them first. Everybody's counting on you.

The roar of the motorcycle gave away the enemy's position. He was trying to swing around to the side of the house and take a new angle, perhaps wing shots through the front obliquely and beyond the dubious cover behind which Matthew sheltered. He fired the Circuit Judge several more times, reaching out of the front of the house as far as he dared, feeling exposed and vulnerable. Finally, the rifle clicked empty.

He ducked back down. Hands trembling, he opened the revolving rifle's cylinder and popped the empty shell casings out. The pouch on the weapon's buttstock held extra cartridges. He slid them in, almost dropping one in the process. The motorcycle engine was closing in again when finally he slammed the cylinder shut and rose to one knee to shoot again.

The biker was right there. He pointed a black pistol of some kind. The muzzle flared orange and Matthew knew there were bullets burning the air to either side of his head.

He pulled the trigger as quickly as he could. He emptied the Circuit Judge in a furious volley. The man on the motorcycle flinched and poured on the speed, peeling out on his big Harley and roaring away from the house. Two other bikers fled with him. One of them threw Matt the finger as they rumbled away. At least one of them was cradling a bloody arm.

Suddenly he felt cold. His whole body was reeling from the adrenaline dump. His ears rang from the gunshots.

Matt looked down at his hand. It was covered in snow. Was it cold enough to snow out? He looked at his arms and then back inside the house. Carol was there with a fire extinguisher, killing the flames. She had sprayed his legs.

"Your pants were on fire," she said, her eyes wide.

Matt stuck his head out of the gap in the window boards and was violently sick.

Chapter 10

"There's another one," said Carol from the back seat.

Matt nodded. He slowed the Subaru, flinching as he did so. He had burned his left forearm badly with propellant gases expelled by the Circuit Judge. It was a design flaw of the short-stocked revolving rifle. If your support arm was not held just so, it could catch the burst of gases from the fired cartridges, which escaped around the cylinder of the weapon when it was fired.

Ahead, the road was blocked by two vehicles — one an overturned pickup truck, the other a burned-out SUV. He wondered if the truck had been damaged and then caught fire, or deliberately torched. Slowly he guided the Subaru around the obstacles, careful to avoid anything that might damage a tire. He had a full-sized spare attached to the roof rack of the car, but he did not even want to think about how vulnerable they would be if they had to stop to change a flat.

In the back seat of the Subaru, Melissa rode in her car seat, talking quietly to Car Bunny, the stuffed rabbit Matt kept in the car for her. Fortunately, he always kept a "kid's survival pack" in the car full of games and toys to keep Melissa busy. Some of it was a little dated; a few of the items were toys she had played with at three and four, but which held less interest for her now.

Carol and Jennifer rode on either side of the car seat. Carol cradled her shotgun in her arms. It was loaded, but not chambered, the barrel pointed toward the window. Jennifer had protested this measure loudly, but Carol wouldn't budge and, being Jen's older sister and not her husband, she won the argument. The Circuit Judge, back in its chair bag, was resting on the floor jutting between Carol's knees. He had not spoken to her when he put it there, but Carol had met his eyes and nodded; she knew he was placing it in back to keep it out of Kepler's hands.

Kepler was back to sullen silence. He had retrieved his trusty iron pipe and propped it near his legs by the door. He had mumbled an apology to Matt, both last night and again this morning, when the adults (except for Kepler) had made the decision to return to Matt and Jennifer's home. They had ample supplies there, hidden in the storage area off the safe room. They just had to get there and ride it out.

"Authorities emphasize that under no conditions are citizens to be on the roads," intoned the announcer.

"Anyone found on the street is subject to arrest."

"Matt," said Jennifer from the back seat. "Are we in trouble?"

"Daniel and I saw police yesterday," said Matt. "Look at these streets. There are too few of them to patrol everywhere effectively, and they'll be focused downtown, probably, supporting the National Guard to quell the civil unrest."

"That poor woman," said Jennifer. "I can understand why everyone's so angry." She looked out the window again. "All these damaged and abandoned cars. Where is everyone?"

"Hiding inside," said Matt. "Just like we are. Except the ones that aren't."

The thought of looters and rioters brought to mind the close calls of the previous day and night. Matt suppressed a shudder. They were doing well so far. They were making good time; they had seen no police, and no one had challenged them. All they had to do was get home, and then they could ride out whatever this was.

The one thing the radio reports could not tell them was what was causing the blackouts, or why it was so widespread. There had been plenty of theories floating around during the course of the summer, from an overworked, overloaded grid, to as-yet-undiscovered terrorism, to solar flares, to any of several other ideas — some bizarre, some not.

"Are we almost home, Daddy?" asked Melissa.

"We're just a few blocks away, sweetie," said Matt. "Don't worry. We'll be there soon."

Kepler, in his seat, perked up. "Hey," he said. "Hey, look. Is that... is that what I think it is?"

Matt's eyes widened. Ahead of them in the road, walking down the middle of the street, were an elderly couple. The man was pulling a two-wheeled cart, of the type people used to do shopping on foot.

"I think I know them," Matt said, squinting. "Isn't that... Jennifer, isn't that the Goldsteins? from over on Porter Street?"

"I think it is," she said.

Matt pulled up alongside the two and rolled down his window. It was the Goldsteins.

"Herman," said Matt. "Herman, it's Matt Avery. Are you all right?"

Herman Goldstein looked blankly at Matt before recognition flashed across his face. "Matthew?"

"Are you hurt?" Matt asked. You don't look well. Mrs. Goldstein, are you okay? Alice?"

"We..." said Mrs. Goldstein. "Our house. It burned down. It burned down."

"We called 911," said Mr. Goldstein. "They put us on hold."

"No one came," said Mrs. Goldstein.

Matt put the Subaru and Park and climbed out. "Come on, you two. You're coming home with us. We'll help you."

Kepler got out of the car. "How are we going to fit

everyone in?"

"It's just a couple of blocks more," said Matt. "We'll take the car seat and put it in the back."

"Matt, that isn't safe," Jennifer complained.

"It's not far," said Matt. "I'll go slow. We need to make room. Kepler can ride in the way-back."

"What?" Kepler asked.

"Mr. and Mrs. Goldstein can fit in the back with you Jennifer, and Melissa can sit on your lap. Carol can ride shotgun up front with me. Literally."

"Maybe I don't like that idea," Kepler said.

"What?" Matt asked.

"Do you really think we can afford to take on more dependents?" Kepler asked.

"We don't want to make any trouble," said Mr. Goldstein.

"You're not," said Matt. "You're coming with us and I won't hear otherwise."

Kepler rapped his metal pipe in the palm of his hand. "This isn't a good idea," he said. "It's not a good idea at all." His eyes met Matt's.

Hefting the pipe, he took a step forward.

Chapter 11

Herman Goldstein kissed his wife's hand and made sure she was comfortable on the couch. Then he went to the dining room and, very carefully, lowered himself into a chair across from where Matt sat, cleaning his Circuit Judge. In one of the recliners in the living room, Kepler snored loudly. Carol, Melissa, and Jennifer were asleep in the home's bedrooms.

"You should get some sleep, Matthew," he said.

"I could say the same for you, Herman," said Matt. "You must be exhausted."

"I am an old man," said Herman. "I do not sleep very much even at the best of times."

Matt paused. He took the bore brush from the open cylinder of the Circuit Judge and looked Herman in the eyes. "I'm sorry about your home," he said.

Herman waved a hand. "I don't care," he said. "We

haven't redecorated in thirty years. I was tired of staring at the same colors." More seriously, he added, "I care nothing for the possessions we lost. We have insurance. We have savings. But if my wife had been hurt or killed..."

"I know what you mean," said Matt. His stomach grumbled. Flushing slightly, he said, "I'm sorry dinner wasn't more substantial. We don't have much in the cupboards."

"Nobody does," said Herman. "Kinda funny when you think about it. We live day to day, believing we will always be able to go to the market, call for take-out. We become outraged if our daily routines are disturbed even for a few hours. People have no idea how close they are to losing everything. We have seen it this summer. Our city is destroying itself. The order we take for granted is collapsing. Well, guess it's not so funny after all, eh?" He nodded to the carbine. "I have never seen a gun a like this."

"It's based on a popular revolver," said Matt. "An ugly, oversized thing called the Judge. It can fire either a .410 shotgun shell or .45 Long Colt ammunition because the two are the same diameter. This is basically just the handgun with a longer barrel and a shoulder stock."

"That stock looks very short," said Herman. "It cannot be comfortable for a man of your size."

"It isn't," said Matt. "And I burned my arm badly when I fired it. Gas from around the cylinder. I held my arm too high, too near the frame."

Herman reached into his waistband, under his button-down shirt, and produced a Walther P38 pistol. Matt's eyes widened as Herman placed the gun on the table. It looked very old. Its finish was worn off in many places.

"I was a boy during World War II," said Herman. "My father took this gun from a German soldier. He told me exactly where, but I have forgotten."

"Does it work?" Matt asked.

"Oh yes," said Herman. "It fires. It is very accurate. I have kept it all these years because my father warned me. He told me that there would come a day when they try to kill us again. Jews, I mean. I do not think he believed society could fall apart, even for a little while, unless there was war. But the idea is the same. This gun twice saved Alice and I from those... those brigands out there. The looters. But you cannot take shelter under a pistol. You cannot eat bullets."

Matt stared at the table. "Herman, I—"

"I am sorry," said Herman. "I meant no criticism. You have done so much for us. You should not torture yourself over the theft of your goods."

"We need supplies," said Matt, looking up again. "I'm responsible. Obviously I didn't safeguard the cache well enough. But I have a plan. And now that I know you have that," he nodded to Herman's pistol, "maybe you can help me."

"I will do whatever I can."

"I have a locker," said Matt. "At one of those self-storage places. It's across town, by design. I keep another cache of supplies there. Food, ammunition, batteries. That kind of thing."

Herman's eyes narrowed. "You are a smart young man," he said. "How did you know you would need these things?"

"I didn't," said Matt. "I hoped I wouldn't. But having a survival kit here, having one in the car and at work... it isn't enough. You've got to have another site, preferably in a different part of the city compared to the others, as a backup in case of emergencies. Originally I thought I might need the storage locker if we were cut off from home. Now it may be our only chance."

"You intend to go after these supplies? Out there?"

"Yes," said Matt. "I don't like it. Jennifer won't like it. I hate to leave them. But I need to keep everyone safe and together while Daniel and I go after the cache."

Herman turned to regard Kepler, sleeping on the couch. "Where did you find this one?"

"We work together."

"He strikes me as a schmuck," said Herman.

"That's not too far off," said Matt. "But I won't leave him behind anymore than I would you and your wife. It wouldn't be right."

"You are a good man, Matthew."

"Herman," said Matt, "Will you keep your gun with you and protect my family, with Carol, while Daniel and I go after the supplies?"

"Perhaps you should take Carol with you," said

Herman. "I will gladly watch over your wife and daughter. And my own Alice."

"I don't want to split us up any more than necessary," said Matt. "I would go myself, but I don't want to leave Kepler here alone. We almost got into a fight at Carol's house. He's volatile. Bad temper. And I think he's just a little too eager to forget about civilization if he thinks there are no consequences for his actions."

"We are what we do when we think no one is looking," said Herman.

Matt nodded. "I can't trust him. But if I just kick him out, I'm no better than the people who fire-bombed Carol's living room."

"Did she lose her house?" Herman asked.

"No," said Matt. "At least... we were able to put out the fire. She had a fire extinguisher handy."

"So few people do, these days," said Herman. "I think even the most basic precautions are a lost concept to most people."

"I hate to think what has happened since we left," Matt said, nodding once more. "As soon as it gets light, I'm taking Kepler with me and going for the supplies. I just need to talk to Jennifer, say good-bye to Melissa, and make sure Carol understands. How much ammunition do you have?"

"Five rounds," said Herman.

"Carol has a few extra shotgun shells," said Matt. "But that's not much. Fortunately I have nine millimeter rounds in my storage area, in a sealed metal tin. A 'survival pack' I bought online."

"But you do not own a nine-millimeter gun, do you?" Herman asked.

"No," Matt said. "But I figured bullets would be the new currency if things fell apart. A good trade item. And you never know what weapons you might find. Nine millimeter is extremely common and very popular with civilian shooters. It's also standard for military handguns these days."

"Not sure how you know all these things Matt…but I'm sure glad you do." Herman said. Lowering his voice, he became gravely serious. "Be careful out there with that one," he said, inclining his head toward Kepler. "He is dangerous. I see it in his eyes. He has a mean soul, a vicious personality."

"I'll be careful," said Matt.

Neither man saw Kepler, only pretending to sleep now, watching them from the living room through slitted eyelids.

Chapter 12

The Subaru moved slowly through the street, dodging everything from burning tires to other, wrecked vehicles. The sirens had stopped in the distance, finally, not because emergency services personnel weren't needed, but because — according to the news — people had started taking shots at ambulances, fire trucks, and police cars. At least one police officer had been killed when his car was swamped by a mob. That hadn't even been in downtown. It had been uncomfortably close to Carol's neighborhood.

Kepler had managed to work his way out of his sullen funk, for which Matt was grateful. As Matt drove, Daniel kept watch out the window, making "guns" with his fingers and tracking the various figures running down the street.

"There's another one with a stolen television," said Kepler. "Can you beat that? What's he gonna do with a TV? There's still no power to most of the city."

"Looting knows no logic," said Matt.

"You sound like that old fossil Goldstein," said Kepler.

"He's a good man."

Kepler snorted. Then he pointed forward. "You better turn up ahead. It looks like it's cut off here." Several burned-out cars were parked across the road, close enough to each other that the Subaru would not be able to get through. The houses on either side were too close, or he would have simply taken the Subaru through the grass on either side. He had defaced too many lawns to think about already that morning. He was grateful for the vehicle's all-wheel-drive.

The right turn was a dead end, or so the street was marked. Matt took the left, a blind corner leading through a twisting city lane. Only when they had passed several houses did Matt realize his mistake.

The National Guardsmen at the roadblock ahead saw them and put out there hands, demanding they stop. They stood next to a desert-sand-color Humvee.

We were too lucky for too long, Matt thought. This was bound to happen. He rolled down his window. Kepler did the same.

"Step out of the vehicle, sir," said one of the Guardsmen. There were only two of them, neither one more than twenty years old. They carried M16 rifles slung over their shoulders.

"You realize you're not supposed to be out on the road, don't you?" said the other.

"We're just trying to get home, officer," Kepler lied, climbing out of the Subaru.

"Do you have any weapons in the vehicle, sir?"

"No," said Kepler.

"Yes," said Matt.

The two Guardsmen looked at each other. Finally, one of them asked Matt and Kepler to stand by the Humvee, where he kept watch over them. The other began going through the Subaru. It did not take him long to find the Circuit Judge. He walked over with the carbine in the crook of his arm.

"I'm required to confiscate this," said the Guardsman, almost apologetically. "We have orders to take all weapons off the street until this unrest has passed. There's been too much violence."

"But that's my property," said Matt. "The carbine isn't illegal. I'm not required to have a permit to keep that."

"And I apologize, sir, but we do have our orders," said the Guardsman. "And, technically, you're not supposed to carry a loaded rifle or shotgun in a moving vehicle per state law, which gives me all the grounds I need to take this. You're free to go, sir, as long as you go straight home and stay off the streets. I can write you out a receipt for this if you want, which will allow you to—"

"You son of a bitch," said Kepler. He took a step forward.

"You stay where you are," said the second Guardsman. "Unless you want to end up in a holding cell until this is all over."

"NOW!" shouted Kepler. "Get 'em, Matt!"

Matt froze, looking on in horror. Kepler did not wait to see what Matt would do. He threw himself at the closer of the two soldiers, grabbing him around the waist and pulling him to the ground. The other Guardsman, still holding the Circuit Judge, tried to juggle the rifle while trying to unsling his M16. In the heat of the moment it never occurred to him simply to use the weapon already in his hands.

Daniel Kepler managed to rip the Kevlar helmet from the Guardsman's head — just before he smashed the man's head violently to the curb.

The other Guardsman dropped the Circuit Judge. It rattled on the pavement. He had his M16 in shaking hands and was starting to bring the barrel up... and in line with Matt's face.

Kepler scooped up the Circuit Judge and smashed it across the Guardsman's face. He fell like a sack of wet grain. Matt managed to lunge forward and catch him before he, too, cracked his skull on the asphalt."

"What are you doing?" Matt demanded. "You could have killed these two!"

"Not for lacking of trying," said Kepler. "I'll do better next time."

"Are you crazy?" demanded Matt. These are American soldiers! They were just doing their job. We could have let them take the rifle. It isn't worth killing anybody over!"

"And what do you think would happen to us if we let them have the gun?" Kepler demanded. "It's our only defense! What will you do when they start coming house to house, taking the guns that are there, too? Do you think Carol would just hand over her shotgun? Do you think any of these National Guard pukes will be there in the middle of the night when looters come to firebomb your home? You think home invaders are gonna care that you obeyed authority and gave up your gun when they bust in to rape your wife and her sister?" He bent and put the Circuit Judge on the ground so he could search the two soldiers.

"Get in the car, Daniel."

"They've got things we can use," said Kepler. His back was to Matt as he said it. "We should take their rifles."

"I said get back in the car!" Matt demanded. "Leave those guns there. We're getting out of here, and we're not going to commit any more crimes while we do it. We have to get to the supplies and get back to my family."

Kepler shrugged. He climbed back into the Subaru. Matt did the same, keeping the Circuit Judge on his lap as he started the car. As they were pulling away from the roadblock and the two unconscious Guardsmen, he prayed neither man would die from his injuries.

He looked down at the carbine as he drove. It was badly scratched from its collision with the pavement. The front sight also appeared to be bent, but he wasn't sure. He would have to examine it carefully when he had the chance.

"You're weak, Matt," said Kepler. "I suspected before,

but I'm sure if it now. You think you're some survival expert. You think you're prepared. But you don't have the guts. You're not mentally equipped to survive. You think there are still rules."

Matt looked to Kepler and opened his mouth to reply.
Kepler was pointing a Beretta M9 pistol at him.

Chapter 13

"I told you those guys had things we could use," he said. "Give me the rifle, Matt, and stop the car. Do it very carefully. You get killed or arrested trying for your cache of supplies if you want to. I'm going my own way before you become an even bigger liability than you already are."

"You can't do this," said Matt. He stopped the car. "I thought we were…"

"Friends?" Kepler laughed. "No you didn't. And I never liked you, either. Now get out."

"Don't do this, Daniel. We can accomplish more together."

"Because you're the Mister Wizard of survival?" demanded Kepler. "Up yours, Matt. I'm so sick of you. I tell you what. In deference to the fact that we've worked next to each other all these years, I won't just shoot you with your own gun and leave your body here to rot."

He drove away.

Matt stood in the middle of the deserted street.

Now what? he thought. Another mistake, and now I'm stranded.

He sat down on the curb. When things go horribly wrong, he reminded himself, don't stand there freaking out. Calm yourself, assess the situation, and then formulate a plan.

He did not dare wait long. They weren't far enough from the National Guard roadblock for his liking; he did not want to end up arrested for Kepler's assault. He also knew, as Kepler did not, that he was actually quite close to the Self Storage unit where his cache was located.

He would walk to the storage area. Then he would find a way to transport home as many of the supplies as he could. Kepler... Kepler could go to hell. If the phone service ever came back, he would report the car stolen, and then Kepler could add Grand Theft Auto to his list of crimes.

His thoughts swam as he walked the rest of the distance. He should have obeyed the nagging voice at the back of his mind, should have cut Kepler loose long before, maybe even left him at the office. Stress did funny things to people, especially if they thought they wouldn't have to pay for their misdeeds. The blackouts, the riots tearing the city apart... they made Matt want to safeguard his family, but apparently they made Kepler desperate simply to protect his own skin.

Next time, he told himself, just be rude. You can't have anyone in your party you can't trust.

His throat was dry. He knew better than to ignore it. There were famous stories of people who died in the desert with water still in their canteens. But what could he do?

He passed a burned out convenience store and gas station. Part of the building still stood, and the label on the door was unmistakable.

LADIES, it said.

The interior of the store was a charred mess, but he found a soot-covered soda can. It was empty. He brushed it off as best he could and then carried the can into what was left of the ladies' room. The door had been kicked in previously, so the lock was not a problem.

He went to the toilet, removed the cover, and was pleased to see there was still water in the toilet tank. While drinking from the bowl was not out of the question, the water in the tank was far cleaner, and still potable fresh water. Too many people ignored water sources like these because of the obvious association. He drank from the tank using his soda can as a cup, then filled the can to carry some water with him.

The water made the rest of the walk easier.

When he finally reached it, the self-storage place was as deserted as the streets had been. The gates were supposed to be locked during non-business hours, but the padlock had been broken and lay on the ground atop a pile of chains. A couple of the storage areas had been busted open, and as he passed, he could see the contents were strewn about. The too-familiar feeling of sickening fear returned to the pit of his stomach.

He almost cried out in relief when he saw his own locker still intact, its lock in place and untouched.

"Hey buddy," said a voice behind him. "You got something good in there?"

Matt reacted on instinct. As he turned to face the speaker, he yanked the bandanna full of batteries from his pocket. In a single, fluid motion, he smashed the man in the side of the face with his homemade sap. The man, perhaps thirty and dressed in mismatched camouflage fatigues, howled in pain and held his face.

Some part of Matt was horrified at what he was doing, but the rest of him was desperate. He could not afford to have his supplies taken, not again. He would not permit himself to become a victim. His wife, his daughter, his sister-in-law, the Goldsteins... they all needed him. They needed the things he was going to bring them.

"Get out of here!" Matt shouted. He smashed at the man's head again as his would-be-attacker tried to shield himself with his arms. "Go! Get out! GET OUT!"

The man in the fatigues finally bolted and ran, just as the bandanna pulled free of its knot and batteries went everywhere. As Matt watched, the man ran past a compact pickup truck now parked at the entrance to the self-storage place. He did not try to get into the truck, instead opting to keep going on foot. Matt was breathing heavy and shaking from the adrenaline dump as he watched the man flee.

He willed himself to keep going, despite how sick he felt. First, he went to the pickup. Wires dangled from its steering column, the collar of which had been smashed free. He had read about this. One set of wires had been stripped and twisted together; that would be the truck's power, to run the lights and the other electrical equipment like the radio. Two more stripped wires dangled freely. Those would be the ignition wires. He climbed in and stroked the two wires together. The engine caught and rumbled to life.

Steadying his trembling hands on the steering wheel, he drove the pickup to his storage area. Then he climbed out, opened the locker, and began emptying his supplies. From the small gun safe he kept in the locker, he removed a Remington 870 pump shotgun, to which a shoulder-sling with bandolier loops full of shotgun shells was attached.

The twelve-gauge rounds were all slugs. He did not dare use anything else, given how unpredictable the spread of the shot could be. He paused only long enough to load the shotgun, then tucked it away inside the cab of his stolen truck.

He was only borrowing the vehicle, he told himself. He did not like it one bit, but his family needed the supplies, and he strongly suspected that his would-be assailant had stolen the truck from someone else. He would take the cache home, unload the truck, and then dump the pickup a few blocks from his house, where hopefully authorities would find it and return it to its owner. That was, unless it was burned like so many vehicles on the street had been. He wondered, briefly, if Jennifer's Hyundai was a smoldering hulk by now.

He put his foot down on the gas.

It was time to make sure his family was safe.

Chapter 14

The Subaru was parked in his driveway.

Matt stopped the pickup three houses down, horrified. If the Subaru was here, that meant that Daniel Kepler must have come back. He could have gained access to the house any number of ways, perhaps by telling Carol and Jennifer that Matt was hurt... or dead. Cursing himself, Matt picked up the shotgun and put it in his lap.

He should have set a verbal password, one that Kepler didn't know. That might have stopped the man from getting in. But it was too late to worry about that now.

Why was Kepler here? The answer was as obvious as Kepler's behavior toward Carol. The man obviously felt he was living, however temporarily, in a world without law. He had made advances on Carol and been rejected. Kepler was just the sort of man to hold a grudge about that... and to come back to settle it.

Matt needed to get inside the house. He needed to do it in a hurry, in a way that would put Kepler off balance and prevent him from mounting an effective counter-assault. The doors would likely be locked. If he paused to fight with them on the way, Matt would be a sitting duck. He put on his seatbelt.

There was only one thing he could think of to do.

He slammed the truck back into drive, mashed his foot on the accelerator, and sent the nose of the pickup truck hurtling toward his own garage door.

The door was reduced to splinters as the pickup careened through it. Matt jammed on the brakes and managed to stop the truck short of the rear wall of the garage. Then he was out and on his feet, headed toward the door to the kitchen. He brought the shotgun up to his shoulder, put the barrel just above the lock of the door, and blew it apart with a single deer slug. Then he kicked the door in and tumbled in behind the shotgun.

"KEPLER!" he shouted.

Gunshots rang out. Bullets struck the wall behind his head. Matt brought the shotgun up again and returned fire, missing Kepler, who was running through the living room. He was firing Herman Goldstein's Walther P-38 as he ran for the hallway to the bedrooms.

Matt racked the pump on his shotgun, fired, racked it again, and fired again. He missed each time. Kepler emptied the P-38 and then threw it at Matt. Matt ducked it.

Kepler slammed the master bedroom door.

The Goldsteins were sitting on the couch, their hands behind their backs. Matt went to them and discovered that Kepler had duct-taped their wrists together. They seemed unharmed, except for the purple bruise below Herman Goldstein's left eye.

"The bastard punched me," said Herman. "He told us you had sent him on ahead to make sure we were safe. I told him I didn't believe him. So he punched me and took my gun. I am an old man, Matthew."

"It's okay," said Matt. "Where is Carol?" He took out his pocket knife and cut the tape on their wrists.

"He's tied her up in your daughter's bedroom," said Mrs. Goldstein. "I think he means to... you know. You stopped him when you crashed into the house."

"And Melissa? Jennifer?"

"In the master bedroom," said Herman. "Hostages, no doubt."

"No doubt. Take this." He handed the knife to Herman. It was a sizable "tactical" model, suitable for self-defense. "Stay here and keep your heads low. There may be... there may be more shooting."

"My ears hurt," said Mrs. Goldstein. "Your gun is loud, Matthew."

"I know, Mrs. Goldstein," said Matt. "I know."

He stood and walked to the hallway. He did not dare check on Carol first. Kepler was in the bedroom with his family, waiting for him. He pressed himself against the wall as tightly as he could, inched down the corridor, and then reached out to rap on the door.

"What?" yelled Kepler. "What do you want, Matt?"

"Let my family go," said Matt. "We have supplies. Things you'll need. You can take them and go. I won't stop you. Just let my wife and daughter leave."

"Deal," shouted Kepler through the door. "But I'm taking Carol with me. I've got your wife and daughter. Don't make me hurt them. Let me walk out of here with Carol and we'll all get what we want."

"No," said Matt. "I won't allow that. I can't."

"Your loss!" shouted Kepler. "I mean it, Matt!"

"Daddy!" shouted Melissa.

"You shut up—" Kepler started to say.

Matt kicked in his own bedroom door, raised the shotgun to his shoulder, and fired.

The slug struck Kepler in the chest. He fell against the bed. A crimson bloom formed on his shirt and spread rapidly. Matt's wife and daughter stood in the far corner of the bedroom, Jennifer protectively sheltering Melissa with her body.

He raised the Circuit Judge and took careful aim.

Jennifer screamed. Melissa buried her face in her mother's chest.

Matt racked the pump of his Remington but knew he would not make it in time. Kepler pulled the trigger.

The bullet struck the wall next to Matt's face.

Matt's second slug tore into Kepler's shoulder. He spun and collapsed to the hardwood floor of the bedroom, only to stagger to his feet again. He came straight for Matt. His face was pale.

"STOP!" yelled Matt.

Kepler didn't seem to hear him. He stumbled past Matt, leaving a bloody trail along the hallway from the bedroom. Matt followed, pointing his shotgun.

"Shoot him!" urged Mr. Goldstein. "Shoot him, Matthew!"

Kepler stumbled through the living room and almost collapsed when he reached the front door. He managed to pull the door open and stumble out.

"I..." said Matt. "I can't. He's unarmed. I can't just shoot a man in the back."

Kepler staggered to the Subaru, bounced off the hood, and hit the driveway heavily. It took him a moment to push himself to his feet again. Matt was standing in the open front door, pointing the shotgun, as Kepler shambled down the street, never looking back. The thick trail of blood he left behind was bright and red in the afternoon sunlight.

A hand touched Matthew's shoulder. He started. It was Mr. Goldstein.

"It's all right," said Herman. "It is over, Matthew. You did fine."

Matt closed the door and leaned against it. He had shot a man. He had probably killed him. Kepler just didn't know he was dead yet.

"Thank you," said Mrs. Goldstein. "Thank you for

what you have done."

"Would someone please come untie me?" yelled Carol from Melissa's room.

Epilogue

The lights were on again, at least for the moment.

They had flickered quite a bit, turning on for an hour and then failing for another. They had been on, now, for at least most of the evening. Jennifer and Carol and been watching the news, while Mr. and Mrs. Goldstein insisted on cooking dinner. Mrs. Goldestein was becoming quite the improvisational cook with freeze-dried foods.

They had all come through without serious injury. In Matt's case, the sights being off on his own Circuit Judge had probably saved his life. They had managed, despite everything. But at what cost?

Matt's five-year-old daughter had been in the room when he had shot a man — twice. The stress and strain of everything they had experienced had taken a toll. Melissa had nightmares when she slept. Jennifer's hands shook as badly as Matt's. Carol was quiet and withdrawn much of the time.

He was more grateful than ever for the steadying influence of the Goldsteins, who had been through so much in life that they were managing to take even this in stride. They had each other, and that was what mattered to them. Matt knew that this was all that mattered to him, too. His family was safe and he was with them. That was a victory.

The news, and the footage on the television, was not good. The city was tearing itself apart. Arson was becoming a daily occurrence. Hundreds of cars had been burned. Looters and wilding thugs, not to mention gangs, were circulating through the city.

The crisis was not over yet. Far from it.

Matt went to the window. He had boarded all of them up, using pieces of the garage door, leaving gaps to keep watch on the street and the back yard. Now, as he had each of the three previous nights, he watched the neighborhood as the sun set. Somewhere in the distance, a car alarm wailed. It was joined by the sound of a fire engine.

A National Guard Humvee roared by. The thought of those National Guardsmen Kepler had left unconscious made Matt feel sick again.

Matt had tried calling the police. They had brushed him off, promising to send someone to take a statement. No one had come yet. He knew they had much more urgent problems to deal with.

So did Matt.

Three days ago, Jennifer had admitted to him that she thought perhaps she was the reason their safe room had been raided. She had spoken of Matt's "prepper illness" at the block party last spring. She had said she loved her husband, but that he was a little paranoid, making a joke of the supplies Matt had stockpiled in their home.

Someone had listened and remembered. Someone, one of his neighbors, had stolen into his house and taken the things his family needed most to survive. The news had hit him harder than the knowledge that strangers, looters, were attacking houses at random. Violent strangers he could understand, after a fashion. But his friends? The people whose children played with his at the local playground? People whose parties he attended?

Matt stood at the window for a long time, wondering why so few of his fellow citizens could be trusted. When he grew tired of his nightly vigil, he would return to cataloging his store of supplies... and refining his plans. There was a lot of work ahead, for all of them.

They were going to have to do a lot better, make a lot fewer mistakes, if they were going to survive.

Made in the USA
San Bernardino, CA
11 December 2013